I0537574

Silenced

By

Author Susan Collins

Copyright © 2015 BTD Group

All rights reserved.

ISBN: 0692504842

ISBN-13: 978-0692504840

DISCLAIMER

This is a work of fiction. Names, characters, businesses, places, events and incidents are either the products of the author's imagination or used in a fictitious manner. Any resemblance to actual persons, living or dead, or actual events is purely coincidental.

i

ACKNOWLEDGMENT

Without you by my side none of this would be possible.
You have given me strength and courage to move
forward in pursuing my dreams, and for that I am
eternally grateful.
I love you beloved.
-Susan

January 1st should have been a holiday full of festive lights, sounds, and cheer, because that was the day that I took my first breath. I was born as Lana Marie to Leigh Lee and David Thompson. I was a healthy bouncing baby girl. It was a warm summer's night.

Some people say they could remember everything about their childhood, the seconds, or even the hours, leading up to their birth. I have always wondered about that, but I can't. Therefore, I have to start from where I can remember and go from there.

My life started at the age of four, in a small town in Kentucky. The population back in those days was around nine thousand, approximately. Still, the town was the biggest city that anyone could ever live in, or so it seemed at my age. There were small gravel roads and not much pavement. Most of the cars were old and rusty.

The buildings were primarily wood. You would only see the brick structures when you had to go downtown to pay bills on the first of the month. However, what could I expect? I was just a four year old little girl. I didn't think or truly care about anything, because my world was *390 Newburgh Street*.

Newburgh Street wasn't just an ordinary street. It was the street with a house on it that I called my safe haven. There I could go find my little cubbyhole, where no one or nothing could hurt me. I have many fond memories of this house and street, but that comes later in my story.

My aunt was my mom and my granny was my mom as well. I thought of my uncles as dads. I have always heard that it takes a village to raise a child, and that's what my brother and I had—a village of family. Everyone worked together and made sure we had what we needed.

Back in those days it wasn't about what you wanted, it was only about what you needed.

My granny, my aunty, and my uncles were there to make sure that my brother and I had all that we needed for the most part.

You might be wondering why I am not saying much about my mom. Well, I often tend to think that our mom was just too young to have babies. My granny told me that when my mom got pregnant with my brother, she took my mom and brother into her home to teach my mom how to care for my brother. He was not a special needs baby or anything like that. But since my mom was a first time parent, who was by herself trying to care for my brother, my granny wanted to make sure that she knew everything that there was to know about raising a baby "*properly*.

"That was the type of granny that I had. She was caring and concerned with the well-being of others, not just for herself, not just for her children, and not just for her grandchildren. She showed genuine care and concern for everyone around her.

Being so young and in a troubled marriage, my mom and dad had no idea what they were doing. They ended up not talking to each other, trying to avoid arguments and the beatings. My mom just let my father do what he wanted to do. Until the day came that she thought she had to do what she had to do. I was so young that I had no idea what was going on. The stories came later to me from my granny. But were they the right stories? That is the question that I often asked myself. I had no choice, but to believe what I was hearing. However, I did wonder and miss my dad a lot. You will never know the longing of a girl that misses her father until her father is gone.

One day, my mom took my brother and me down to my safe haven. I just thought that mom had to go somewhere important, and that we had to stay with granny and aunty. I didn't mind, because we were well taken care of there.

I was happy even if we didn't have the biggest house on the street, nor had the prettiest dolls among my friends. My granny and aunty were always there to give us their warm hugs, whenever they came home from work. They would listen to my littlest worries, reassuring me that things happened for a reason.

Looking at the situation now, there was a lot more going on with my mom than I could have ever imagined. Nevertheless, we were at a place where we felt loved. We could see love and never had to wonder what love was, because we knew that we were wanted. Our granny's house was that place.

If we fell off our bikes on the old gravel road, it was because we were riding too close to the edge of the road. When we got hurt physically, or something wrong happened to us, it was because of us being playful kids and nothing else. When, or if we were bit by a spider, or stung by a bee, it was because we were hard-headed little ones, who didn't listen when granny said, "Don't go outside messing with that big beehive and don't bother something that doesn't bother you."

We didn't listen, and often we did the complete opposite of what she said. But when those "bad" things happened, guess what we did? We went running to granny or aunty for them to heal our boo-boos, crying as if the world was coming to an end, or the sky was falling down. With tears running down our cute little faces, who could be mad at us? But we had been warned and didn't listen.

I silently chuckle inside and smile as I think of those days. They were filled with a child's innocence.

Those were simple times on an old street, in a small town, in a house I called "love." This house was all wood without insulation to shield us from the cold winter months in Kentucky, so as to keep the wind out. I remember when granny put some old clothes and newspapers in some of the cracks. It helped deter some of the cool breezes.

But in Kentucky, it gets bitterly cold, so cold that I would rather hold my pee all night long then get out of bed to go to the bathroom. Have you ever been so cold that you could hear your teeth in your sleep? I have, and when it was just that cold, I always felt the cozy and warm arms of my aunty surrounding me.

Sometimes during the winter time in this house, the wooden floors would freeze making them slippery. When that happened, granny or aunty would give us two pairs of socks to put on our feet, to make sure that our feet stayed dry and as warm as possible. That was just during the winter time. We did not complain.

The summer was a butterfly of a totally different color. As the sun was at its highest point in the sky, I remember sweating, as if I just got out of the swimming pool.

There was no air conditioning, just a few very old fans, which fit perfectly in the windows. Sweating was a daily thing back then. Getting darker and thinner was too. As for the darker and thinner part, it was because we were young kids. We were doing what young kids do best in the long hot summer months. Riding our bikes outside was our greatest pastime.

Not only were we giving granny and Aunty'nem a break, but we were having fun. As soon as our eyes opened, we were on our bikes. The uneven, grassy and gravel county roads were our paths for adventure and mystery, like finding a treasure map just without the map. Those were days of unlimited excitement. I felt that was a happy and normal life for children like my brother and me. We were enjoying the country road, racing and getting our clothes dirty. We couldn't resist the mud holes when we came across them.

Popsicles were our best friend, during the sizzling summer months. Our favorite flavors of Popsicles had to be cherry, grape and orange, of course.

But at night, the ungodly blood sucking mosquitoes would almost eat me alive.

Waking up with mosquito bites all over our bodies had to be one of the most unpleasant feelings summertime could offer. We looked like we had the chicken pox, but without actually having them.

Then granny or aunty came with the rubbing alcohol to make the itching feel better. It didn't matter though. I just got up the next morning and started my day all over again. Some things just didn't matter and we believed it was just a "norm" because at the end of the day we were loved.

I could feel the love from my aunty and granny. You probably think that the "norm" isn't being eaten up by mosquitoes, but truth be told, I think that I'd rather be bitten every day by mosquitoes than go and live at my own mom's house.

Oh! But let me tell you about my granny's room. The first room of the house was not the living room.

It was grannies, and she was the guardian and superior safe keeper of the whole house. You had to get past granny in order to get in her room and that was a tough job. Then after careful interrogation, you were given a chance to come in, but it wasn't always easy. I know, because I tried on more than one occasion. Within granny's room was everything a child would want to play with. Everything shined and was very amusing to look at, as they shimmered in your eyes, like a twinkle in a star. Sometimes I just wondered, "How old was this stuff?" I loved it when granny would call me into her room and have me sit down, just to tell me stories about her life.

My granny did not have an easy life. She grew up picking cotton, being married and raising seven little babies, pretty much by herself. She did what she had to do, like most black women back in those days.

I think—that is what made her such a great protector of her family. She endured so many obstacles and hardships.

I remember one story that she told me about her not having food to feed her babies. It was in the dead of winter, she had an old iron stove that would keep the room warm where the children would sleep. Tackled with the idea that her children were not going to bed hungry, she stole corn and greens from the neighboring farm just to make a meal.

Before she got a chance to fill her hunger, she made sure her children's bellies were filled first, so they could go off to sleep.

I loved it when granny would call me into her room and have me sit down, just to tell me stories about her life. I felt as if she looked at my brother and me the same way. That is why she was and still is one of our protectors.

The porch was also made of wood, and we jumped on it like a trampoline. The wood was so flimsy it was fun to jump on, held together with only a few nails. I'm sure more nails were missing than should have been, because you could hear the wood cracking sometimes when we stepped in the wrong place.

Sometimes the wood broke and we would fall through to the ground. Then everyone came running out of the house to make sure that we were okay. Once they saw that we were fine, they held their laughs in as long as they could, but the big grins and smiles came, and then the laughter.

It wasn't because we fell, but because everyone told us not to jump on the porch in the first place. There were holes in the wood as well. You could literally see the ground underneath.

Every now and then, one of God's creatures would visit us without our approval, and uncle would have to go and get his big shotgun out to kill it.

I remember the old washing machine located in the kitchen. Aunty would open the kitchen door and pull the washing machine around, then get the hose to hook it up. Then with a little prayer it started (yes, it used electricity), but before we got that one, she washed our clothes by hand on a "*wash board*" (I think that's what they called it).

The washing machine did not have a rinse cycle, and there were two rollers on top of it that you would have to put your clothes into, in order to wring the water out of them.

"Wow, aunty, how does this thing do that?" I would ask. Her answer was always the same, "With hard work, Lana.

I have to make sure y'all clothes are clean, right? So it takes hard work, because I can't have my little girl walking around with dirty clothes on, now can I?"

I remember wearing jeans during the winter and then cutting them off for shorts in the summer. This made it easy to find an outfit that matched, and at least it fit the season. I guess some would say that we were poor, but I didn't think so.

In the backyard were a few cows, a few goats, a lot of chickens and pigs. In addition, we had dogs, cats, rabbits, deer, and rows of veggies.

I remember having to get up early in the morning to go out to the chicken coop and gather the eggs for breakfast. We never got them all, only a few, because granny always made sure that some were left in the coop. That way the eggs would hatch and we would always have chickens.

The pigs smelled just plain terrible, and I never really understand how such a smelly, big-eared pig could taste so good. I remember when it was time to kill one of the pigs (No, "hogs" was what it was called, because a pig was the little one). There was a big, really big black pot and a huge fire and a thing that looked like a *"hangman game,"* that was put up with the ropes, and plenty of knives, water, one shotgun, and a shell. My uncle would shoot the hog in its head, after that, cut its throat. Finally, he hung it upside down by its tendons. It was a very grim sight, blood was everywhere, and the hogs didn't always die quickly.

Some would buck and squeal, with blood running out of their mouth. When finally it was over, it was on its way to hog heaven. We prayed, thanking God for providing us with the meat to feed our family.

We also gave meat to other families, so that they too could have food for their children. Now our freezer was full and granny was happy. We were not rich in money, but we were rich in all other ways. My aunt and granny made sure my brother and I were cared for in every way they knew how.

Now as I look back, I don't think my mom was ready to be a mom when my brother or I were born. She was young, but not as young as most people back in those days.

During school time I remember my aunt coming to the table to help my brother and me with our homework, after she came home from work.

I also remember my granny coming in from work, cooking dinner, filling up our plates with enough food to feed four other kids. We had to eat it all. Boy, those were the days.

That was my childhood, filled with love, unconditional love, like no other, the love of my family. These were the days that I will always look back on and cherish forever in my memories.

At the age of ten, I started wondering "Who am I?" "Where did I come from?" "Where's my dad?" "Why doesn't he show up?" "Where's my mom and why isn't she here with us?" These were just questions that surrounded my mind.

I never thought that, if I put the questions out into the universe, that one day the universe would answer them back. But it did. She showed up and took us away, away from everything that we had known and everything that we loved. Our little world was crumbling down, and I began to rebel. Who is she? "*Your mom*, "replied Granny.

Just who does she think she is, taking me away from my aunt, my granny, my uncles, and my family to come live with her? I began to think to myself. Still, the love of my aunt followed and she came with us as well. I think my aunt loved my brother and me, like we were her own children. Still to this day I feel that way.

It was depressing because my mom took us away from our home. She took us away from what was normal. I rebelled. I thought how could my brother and I feel loved?

Suddenly, school wasn't so much fun anymore and I hated to attend. I felt like an outsider. My grades began to drop as well. I started angrily fighting, trying to fight my way back to my granny's house in the country.

By doing this, I thought my mom would send me back to my granny's. But it did not work. What ended up happening was terrible. My mom, out of confusion or desperation, hit me, slapping me and on some instances beating me up.

She could not handle my sudden shift in attitude. She did not want to understand that I would rather be with granny and aunty than with her. There were a lot of nights that I cried and begged God to please take me away from my mom. Please somehow make my granny come and get me. I didn't want to live there I wanted to go back to the home I had known.

I didn't want to live in the uptown part of Mountain View Urbandale, in *apartment 505* in the Midstream Projects. My mom worked at *Russell's Family Store*, a small store around the corner from the house.

I had my aunt, who would come over to make sure Andre and I were alright and to tell us that she loved us. My mom was hardly ever there. My aunt caring for my brother and I seemed to bring a strain between my mom and their relationship, so my aunt left.

Later there was a conflict between them. My mom was jealous, since my brother and I listened to our aunt rather than her. One of the women we knew as a mom had left us, in a way of speaking, to save us. But I am far from being saved.

My mom had a boyfriend, and I hated this man because he looked at me strangely, and I felt awkward when he was around. Some days he looked at me like I was meat, or a worm on a hook. My stomach was always in knots when he was there. If he was in one room, I made sure that I was in the other.

If he called my name, I made sure that my brother went with me just to see what he wanted.

When granny would come over, I could hear her tell mom, "Stop leaving your children with that man," I wish mom would have listened. Unfortunately mom didn't listen and left us there with him all the time, because she had to work. *Oh, would I have loved to be with my granny.*

I did not want to understand and the uncomfortable feeling was always there. The feeling of a lion waiting patiently, to pounce.

Now I was eleven, it was a hot summer day of playing. Mom had called from work and said my brother and I needed a bath before she got home. Because of the playful kids that we were, neither one of us wanted to go inside the house to take a bath.

My brother and I were still outside. Mom's boyfriend said that I should go and get my bath out of the way. I ran my water and gathered my clothes. I went into the bathroom and closed the door. I thought that the door was locked, but it wasn't.

The door opened slowly, I called out, "Momma is that you?" But there was no answer. I put the wash towel close to my chest, "Andre is that you? Stop playing around!" But there still was no answer. I started to shake, getting frightened, as the door continued to creak open. The hand that rounded the door made it obvious who was at the door. It was my mom's boyfriend.

I yelled, *"I'm in here"*, *"I'm in here."* *"Andre come here, Andre come here please, Andre!"* But he could not hear me plead. He was still outside.

He didn't know I was inside the house having my bath. I laid in the bath tub, waist deep in the water with a small towel covering my bare chest. I crossed my legs.

Then I asked *"What are you doing? Get out of here. I am going to tell my mom."*

He replied, "Who will she believe?"

"Andre! Andre! Andre! Andre," I shouted.

"There's no need to keep calling your brother. He can't hear you, he's outside playing." he tells me.

Tears flowed down my face.

"Please get out!"

Then he begins to touch my boyish chest and tell me how good it made him feel. His hands were like burning charcoal as it touched my tiny fragile body. It burned so much that I wanted him to stop.

I wanted him to leave me alone.

Then he asked me *"Doesn't that make you feel good?"*

I wept for my brother. I cried uncontrollably. I begged and pleaded with the devil to please leave the bathroom, but it was to no avail.

He was like a hungry animal pouncing every inch of my body. I wished to God that I was a bigger person, that way I could fight him off, but I could not. He squeezed my little thighs as I begged him again to get his hands off me. The water in the tub swished around like a washing machine while I tried to fight and beg at the same time.

"Please! Please! Please! Stop! Stop! Stop!"

My hands were not big enough to get him off of me. I needed help. As all of this was happening, I asked God to help me.

Then the unthinkable happened. He inserted his hands between my legs.I was weak fighting him off me. I became weaker with the intense pain that he had given me. I felt something inside me break and tear. It was so painful. Then the water went red, my cries turned into a whimper.

That monster just walked in and took my innocence in such a horrible way. All of the things that keep a little girl pure were taken from me that night. Now as I look back, no child should ever be touched that way. No one should ever be touched inappropriately ever.

I saw his evil face with such unimaginable expression, as he stood up telling me that he was done, and that I needed to finish my bath.

He left with a threat saying that I should not mention this to my mom, because my mom would not believe me.

I cried, not because of the physical pain, but because I knew that I was broken.

I locked myself in my bedroom, crying, hurting, bleeding, and wondering why he did this to me. Why? I wouldn't hurt anyone. I would touch nothing. I wasn't being bad. I did as he asked and went to take my bath. Why did he punish me in such a manner? Did I ever do something to deserve this?

Tears rolled down my face uncontrollably, until my mind got tired of thinking and crying. I felt like dozing off a little. I never left my room.

I locked myself inside waiting for my mom while looking out of the window gazing at the stars, but I think that it was more like the stars just happened to be in my sight. I was waiting for the lights of safety, *my mom, I thought*, when I saw the lights of my mom's car.

I ran downstairs to the door crying, with her boyfriend right behind me. Mom just kept asking me, *"Lana what's wrong?"*

I wanted to yell and scream at the top of my lungs and tell her what he did to me, but nothing came out. I was choking inside with anger, with pain and with hatred. I just had this blank look with tears that just wouldn't stop, trying to hold on tight to my mom's hand.

I wanted to say the words, but that monster was trying to pull her into the laundry room. He was pulling her away from me!

Then, out of rage, I was able to speak, crying it all out. I tried to tell her what her boyfriend did to me, wanting her to save me from him, so that he wouldn't do it again. I wanted her to tell me that he did an awful thing. I wanted her to kill him dead for hurting her daughter.

When she understood, everything happened in a split second. She called my granny first, and then she got a gun from her dresser. All I can remember is the bang of the gun, the police, blood and my granny coming through the door rushing, grabbing me, and saving me.

I heard my mom telling me that he would never do it again and that he would never come back. Mom didn't go to jail.

After I spent a week or so at my granny's house, one day my mom showed up and took me away again. I thought this time she would take care of me.

But instead, she questioned me about what happened that night in the bathroom. It was like she didn't believe me, like she was someone else and nothing I said was true. She told me that I was a fast girl trying to be a grown up and that I was only eleven going on twelve.

From her words, it seemed like I acted out on my own seducing her man. My heart was broken. My innocence was lost. How can you question your child when she comes to you with something like this? What did I really do wrong? Why was my mom treating me like this?

I always thought and knew that your mom was supposed to love you, protect you and always be there for you. Am I wrong? Did I miss something? Is this my fault?

"I'm a tomboy, Mom!" I didn't dig boys like that. They were my friends, my playmates. I had a brother, my best friend, someone I lived and played with on a daily basis. You let your boyfriend do this to me, break my innocence! (I thought to myself)

It built such a rage inside of me that I hated life. I could not trust anyone, at least not a man. No man's hand could come close to me, or else I jumped.

Afraid they wanted to do to me what *he* had done.I began to hate them all, and someone so young shouldn't have feelings like this. I hated the life that I had to live with my mom. I didn't feel the motherly love or the motherly touch.

You would think, that with what I just had to endure, that my mom would be understanding, warm, and loving. But my mom was someone so different. She looked at me with disgust in her eyes. She blamed me strongly for that night. She had judged me wrongly for what had happened and just insisted that it was my fault it happened.

Her way of communication was even worse. She would throw things at me, when there were things needed to be done (like laundry or for me to put up clothing). It was the same with Andre.

She would always tell me, *"You aren't shit, but a fast ass little girl."*

A flirt is what I was to her. My mom would call me a bitch, so much that I began to think that she renamed me, say things like

"Oh, so you want to be fucked huh?"

It seemed like she wanted to fight me. She would walk into the room and bump into me and stand there, look at me and say, *"Oh, so you want to hit me now?"*

Even though my response would be *"No,"* the outcome would always be the same. Me running to my room just to get away from her, all the while saying please mom, what did I do to you, for you to hate me so much?

I felt sorry for my brother too, because after mom went into her room, Andre would peek his head into my room and say, *"Lana are you okay?"* I always smiled, and said *"Yes."*

But he knew that was not the case. I could see genuine care and concern for me in his eyes. What could he do though? I did not want for him to suffer and experience the same things.

My brother was the only light I could see from where I was then. He didn't need to suffer like I was.

Deep down inside I longed for *Newburgh Street* even more. I missed my granny. I missed being treated as a family member. I missed being respected as a person by my family.

This went on for weeks and got progressively worse each week. But one day, all of a sudden, my mom was nice to me. I was thinking to myself, is she going to kill me now? What should I do? I did the only thing that I could do. I waited and worried.

It was a big question as it puzzled me, why she was suddenly so good to me. It was such a very unexpected change in her, that there were a lot of sleepless nights, with more crying. I begged God for his help. A child should never have to go through worries like I did.

I was unable to eat, sleep, and bathing was barely an option. I had so much to worry about at a very young age. What I truly needed was the loving touch of my mom. I needed the protection of my mom, none of which were present.

I remember it getting so bad for me that one night when it was late, I went into the kitchen. I walked as if the floors were made of cotton, quietly as possible. I didn't even want to make the tiniest creaking noise. Once I made it into the kitchen, I grabbed the big knife and then returned to my room.

After that, I looked for the perfect hiding spot, thinking to myself, if mom was to grab me, how long would it take for me to get to the knife?

I realized that if she grabbed me, that I would be a goner instantly. The only place for the knife would have to be under my pillow. So there you have it, I kept that knife under my pillow and I slept with one eye open, with one of my little hands on the handle.

Scared out of my own mind, scared of my own mom. I was just a child at such a young age feeling so scared of being home. This should not be.

As time went on, I missed my aunty, and my granny. It felt as if my mom kept me away from them without any reason. They didn't show up as much, and the calls were barely there.

I asked time and time again if I could go back to *Newburgh Street* to spend time with my family, my safe haven, my cubbyhole, my security blanket. When I asked to go, the answer was always *"No."* My mom would even yell with nasty words. It was no use asking her, since she would not really let us go.

A little more time passed, and mom said, *"Come on and let's go."*

I was excited thinking we were going to Newburgh Street and asked, *"Where are we going, mom?"*

She replied *"Out across the river."*

Her answer knocked me down to my spine and I yelled, *"No, please, don't make me go."*

That's where the boyfriend lived with his mom. I felt that I had no choice, and had to go.

Now I knew why she was being good to me. She wanted me to accept this day that I would have to face her monster boyfriend again.

Scared isn't what a child should feel riding with her mom, but I was, and as the roads unwound the house appeared. I became more scared.

I remember looking at this big tree that was in the yard, asking God to save me from anything that might happen to me again, when a single drop of dew fell on my cheek. Being so young I didn't know if it was God, but I felt comfort. If only for that instant, I knew that God was with me.

I got out of the car and went into the house with my mom. I held her hand tight making sure no one would suddenly grab me or pull me away from her.

The inside of the house was darkly lit, and the smell of old-people was all around. When I looked up, the monster was there looking at me. He was on crutches, because my mom had shot him in the leg. I felt guilty, it was my fault

I shouldn't have said anything and because I did, this man suffered. But I suffered more with what he had done to me. I froze for a while with eyes wide open in fear. I held my mom's hand tighter, while she on the other hand was trying to let go as if telling me to go near her monster boyfriend.

When he reached out his hand, as if he wanted to touch me, I jolted. My instinct was to run. I ran, begging my little legs to move faster, to run as if the sky was falling. I needed to hide. I needed my safety place, my cubbyhole, my family, where my aunt might be.

My heart was calling them, please come and save me, my mom took me here to get hurt, please aunty show up and help me.

My heart was pounding so hard out of my chest. I was running as fast as I could down this old dark street that did not have any lights. I didn't want to be found. I'd rather die than go back to that house.

I wished that some wild animal would come across my path, kill and eat me up. That way I wouldn't have to go back to the monster's house.

I covered myself up with as much mud as I could. I kept very still, even holding my breath at times, trying not to be noticed. I didn't care being covered in filthy mud, as long as my mom wouldn't find me. As long as I didn't go back to that monster's house. I didn't want to be near him ever again!

Then my mom came and somehow found me hiding down the street in that muddy ditch. It was a place I thought that she would never look, but she eventually found me.

She pulled me up from the ditch, as I tried to free myself from her grip. The moment she got me out, she slapped me across my face as hard as she could. She had so much anger in her eyes, saying, *"Come on and let's go."*

I didn't have any choice as she dragged me to walk back down that street. I was crying and trying to beg her not to let me near that house, but she was so much stronger than me.

As I rounded the corner, I had a glimpse of our car and it looked like the car was filled with clothes and bags. My heart was racing with dismay.

No, no, no, no! She's bringing him back.

No, no, no, no! I just wanted to die.

Lord let me drop dead now, please God. I don't want him to hurt me, please God. I will be a good girl, I will wash the dishes, I will take out the trash I will not have to be called twice to do a chore, just don't let this man come back to my mom's house. Please! *No, no, no!*

But God didn't seem like he heard me, because that man came back. He came to stay with us again. His presence was a nightmare! In my thoughts, it was better having my mom say all those nasty words to me, at least it was just us in our house. No monster to be afraid of. I was so scared to take a bath and even more scared to be in the same room with him.

Our house became like a lion's lair once again. Where the lion was just sitting around waiting for the chance to attack.I held on to my brother in every way possible.

The only place that I didn't go with my brother was the bathroom. I would always ask him to stay by the door. My mom never even noticed that I didn't sleep in my room anymore, after the monster came back. Instead, I stayed in my brother's room. I even slept on his floor just to feel safe.

One day, though, it was a surprise to all that there came a knock on the door, and it was granny! I was so relieved! The skies opened up and the sun shone down on me, because my granny came to save me. She was like an angel sent from heaven to give light to my dark and scary world.

She and my mom went into mom's room, and the door closed, but I still heard my granny and mom fussing. My granny's tone was high pitched like a cat in a fight.

She asked my mom how she could let this man come back to her house around her daughter, after he did such a thing to her, saying, *"What is wrong with you?"*

Then she said, "If your mom doesn't get rid of him, *I'm going to call the police and the child protective service people and get them to take you away."*

I knew that mom couldn't win over my granny. Granny is one tough momma. Then I guess she looked at the monster. I heard her *say "If you touch my granddaughter again, I will kill you!"*

She went on to say that she wasn't going to shoot him in the leg like my Mom did, but shoot him in the head. She told him that her shotgun was in the trunk of her car and that she should kill him now just in case he had any thoughts of touching me.

Even the monster wasn't able to talk back to my granny, as if a cat got his tongue. I didn't hear him say a word at all.

Again, my granny was my light, and on that day the clouds opened and the sun shined again. I was astonished. Andre grabbed me by the arm and took me into his room.

He closed the door and said, *"Here Lana, I got a knife from the kitchen. If he stays here still, and comes into your room, you stab him. Then come into my room and I will tell the police that I did it. Do you understand me Lana?"* Andre's words were tough and steady.

I nodded and said, "Yes." Then I took the knife and hid it under my pillow. He knew everything now. He had heard what really happened that night and somehow he felt guilty for not being there that day to protect and defend me from the nasty boyfriend.

He blamed himself for leaving me alone with the monster.

Now, I was scared not just for me, but for my brother as well. I was scared about having to deal with mom too.

I asked God to help me, so now can I say that this is help? I don't think that my mom wanted to play around with granny, because she was a one-word woman, and she had respect from all around.

She didn't play with anyone, but said what she meant and meant what she said. I truly believe she would have killed him. I guess my mom was also scared of what my granny could do to that monster. After granny's confrontation with my mom and that monster, he was instantly gone.

But it's too late for me. I am broken and I know for sure that no one can fix me now, or will there be someone who really can?

Though the monster had left my mom's house, my memories still lingered. The awful nightmares had gotten even worse. Closing my eyes and trying to sleep or even have a peaceful dream was almost impossible. I even started to wet the bed from time to time, because I didn't want to go to the bathroom. I had the thoughts of the monster jumping out from the shadows taking a chance to kill me, because of what granny had said to him. It had scared me more.

I knew that no one could really understand what I felt. No one could ever imagine the fear I had inside, but I just wondered why. The months went by, and my birthday was just around the corner.

On July 3^{rd,} the day I was turning 12, mom had to go to work that morning. I was at home with my brother playing outside and trying to listen for the phone to ring. We didn't want to miss it if mom called.

She was just working a few blocks away from our house.

I was playing in the field trying to catch bees, and I had one in my hand. It stung me, and I cried out loud, *"Oo! Oo! Oo! Ouch!"*

Then I was startled that someone grabbed my hand. As I looked up the sun blocked my view, and I put my hand up so that I could see who it was.

The most beautiful face appeared, my beloved aunt, my mom was there.

"Come here, baby," she said, *"Let me see what that bee did to you."* If I knew what heaven looked like, I would definitely say that it was right in front of me at that moment.

We walked back to the house and she doctored my hand, and then she said, *"I have something for you."*

I wondered what, and then she said, *"Did you think I would forget that today is your birthday?"*

She handed me a white box with a red ribbon wrapped around it. I smiled as big as I could. The biggest smile that seems like it could hurt your cheeks for the rest of your life, and I tore the box open. It was a brown shirt trimmed in red.

I loved it, and then my aunty said, *"When I am not here with you and you want me, and you feel scared, put this shirt on, and I am here."*

She hugged me like she used to, a long deep heartfelt hug, and I could feel the love, the warmth of my aunty, my mom. I could hear her heart beat, and for that instance, everything was OK. I was safe, because my aunty made it safe for me again. It was like she brought *Newburgh Street* to me in Midstream Projects.

She brought my sunshine, my light, and it was all wrapped up in this one amazing shirt.I felt so loved that day. I guess I must have worn that shirt every single day. I remember washing it out by hand and laying it on a towel so that it would dry.

I didn't want anything to happen to it. That shirt was nothing Jean. It was not studded with jewels or diamonds, but made with love from my aunty, a beautiful gift given by a beautiful and caring woman.

My life at that point looked brighter. One ray of sunshine beamed down on me day after day. The warmth was given through a very simple shirt and not because it was winter, but because love made it happen. The shirt served as my security blanket all along.

A few weeks later, I woke up from taking a nap late in the evening. My mom was at work. I felt something wet and wondered if I had peed in my clothes. I did that from time to time after that monster hurt me. I ran to the bathroom and I was bleeding.

No, no, no, now what did I do wrong? What's wrong with me? I started screaming for my brother to tell him that I was dying and there was blood in my underwear, *"What to do! What to do! Help me Andre!"*

Seeing me in such a panic, he calmly let me sit down on one side of the tub, and said that it would be okay. He would handle it and that I just needed to stay there and wait for him. He left the house and came back a few minutes later with a bag of Kotex Maxi Pads. I wondered what I was doing with this, but my brother explained to me how to use them.

Then he said to take a bath and do as he had told me. He stood outside of the bathroom door, as if a guard watching over me. Every few minutes he would say, *"Lana are you okay in there?"*

Then I would reply, *"Yeah, I think so, are you sure that this will work and I will be okay?"*

But deep down inside I trusted my brother and I knew that he would not let anything happen to me because he loved his little sister, so I did everything he said.

I felt like a baby because it was like wearing a diaper though it was smaller than a real diaper, but it felt funny. My brother told me that I needed to wear this thing, so I did. My granny came to check up on me too, because my brother called her and told her what had happened to me.

So then granny sat down on the side of the bed with me and explained to me what I was going through and what all of this meant.

"Lana, you're becoming a woman now," she said, but all I could think of was that I didn't want that.

My granny told me that every girl my age will pass this stage to become a woman. I wanted to stay a tomboy. I liked being a tomboy. I liked my jeans, tennis shoes and t-shirts.

Do I have to wear dresses now? I didn't want that. I wanted to be able to play with my brother and his friends in the field.

I wondered who in their right mind would want to become a woman. I still didn't want and couldn't accept that I was becoming a woman as my granny had said. *"No, I don't want it, can you please tell it to go away, granny?"*

But I had no choice because it was my time. No matter how I didn't like it, it was already happening to me.

Then she gave me some pills because my tummy hurt so badly. It was painful, like knives were cutting my insides out.

"Is this what I have to get used to, pain every month? Oh, with this pain, just let me die now and get it over with!"

That's what it felt like. With these words, my granny just laughed at me and gave me a kiss on my forehead.

My brother also, seeing granny laughing, teased me saying that I will forever feel this pain. I gave both of them a silly grin. I was feeling better having my granny and my brother beside me.

Later that night, I remember my mom coming into the room rubbing her hands through my hair and gently asking me if I was OK.

She looked different, her eyes were softer. Her voice seemed sincere and she asked if there was anything that I needed. The look in her eyes was even gentler, not the look that I had become used to seeing from her, and her touch was warm. Was it genuine care and concern or something different?

This is the beginning of young womanhood and with all I have endured this far, I have this curse that visits monthly. I thought that God must really hate me? This is something that I definitely do not want to get used to. But things appear and happen that I have no choice over. I have to grow up. By force!

Finally, when I was twelve years old, I began to be my own little person. My mom even allowed me to cook chicken one day, and I did a great job at it too. The chicken was golden brown and smelled good. I was so proud of myself that day.

It doesn't sound like much, but to a twelve-year-old it was a great feat. I could pick out my own clothes, and life didn't seem so bad. My mom trusted me to do small house chores and I was glad about that. As for that monthly curse, that was still coming around and I was getting used to it, but it was still nasty and hurt a lot. Still, if anyone ever said that becoming a young woman would be easy, they lied.

My brother Andre began to look at me differently though. I often wondered as to why he did that. It was not too much longer before I found out just why.

But let's look back, I was finally in a "happy" place in my life, or I thought that it was a happy place. That is until, one day. Andre wanted to play cards, and there's nothing wrong with playing cards with your brother, right?

But in this instance it was, because usually we would play and bet for cookies or jeans if anybody lost. But this card game was a different one.

My brother said to me, *"If you lose, I get to put my penis in your vagina!"*

I was appalled, *"How could you say that to me."*

You are my brother and brothers are supposed to protect their little sisters. But the look in his eyes weren't ones of protection. It gave me the creeps and an ill feeling deep inside of my stomach to the point where I wanted to vomit.

I told Andre, *"No! I cannot play cards with you and do that. It's wrong, and you want to hurt me like mom-ma's boyfriend did, how dare you even speak to me that way. No, I won't do it."* But he insisted, over and over again.

I walked away from my brother and I could never look at him the same. Just for what he had said to me. All of the broken emotions, the hurt from the sickening actions of mom's boyfriend, everything he had done, everything came back.

I isolated myself into my bedroom for the remainder of that day. Not wanting to eat the chicken that I had carefully prepared and was so proud of.

All of the anxiety had resurfaced. What was I to do? This was my brother! I kept saying to myself. I went to sleep saying the same thing over and over. This is my brother! How can he say that to me?

The next morning, I tried to avoid my brother like he had the plague, but he was Andre. I had to confront him at some point, and confronting him is what I really did.

He was walking out of his room and I was in the living room.

I called his name, *"Andre, can you come here please?"*

Before I could open my mouth again, Andre was apologizing for what he had said to me. I didn't feel easy just because he apologized. There was a vibe in the air that I could feel.

Later that night, Andre came into the kitchen and asked if I wanted to play cards again.

My immediate reply was *"No! Not for that!"* "No, no, no!"

"Lana just cards."

"Are you sure Andre?"

"Yes Lana, I am sure."

I told him that I would only play three games, because I had to bathe, and get ready for bed.

It was like old times, playing cards with my brother, me trying to cheat at the hands and him trying to figure out why I always had so many cards. We laughed and laughed, but at the conclusion, we said *"Good game."*

I went into my room and gathered my clothes, went into the bathroom and started to run my water, but I forgot my socks, so I had to go back to my room. When I opened the bathroom door, Andre was there.

"Hey Andre, do you have to use the bathroom, go ahead I have to go to my room and get my socks. You better not do a number two and leave the bathroom all stinking."

But the look on his face was so unusual. Yet, it still said it all. No words came out of his mouth. He raised back his arm and hit me right in my left eye. I then slammed myself to the floor. My brother was all over me, I wish I was stronger so I could fight, but he was bigger. He could hit harder. When he hit me in the mouth I began to cry.

"Please Andre don't do this! Please Andre, Please don't do this!"

My cries fell on deaf ears. I will never be able to look at my brother the same again. He was my brother, the protector I thought. He was my knight in shining armor, I thought.

But I was wrong, he was just like the rest of them. He was a male and all guys wanted to hurt me. I didn't tell mom. I didn't tell granny nor aunty. I bottled what my brother did to me up inside me.

My brother was not my brother anymore he was just him and now I was just me. I could give no love or respect to him.There were nights that I thought about cutting his throat while he slept, burning his bed or just burning down the whole house, because in my eyes everyone needed to die.

Old emotions slowly resurfaced and I had to put them back in the bottle and pretend nothing was wrong. But everything was absolutely wrong now!

Never ask me to play cards, because the answer will always be, NO! I could never trust him again from that point on. Still to this day the pain lingers just to tell the story of the playing cards. I can never look at a deck of cards the same.

Mom came home with a man, and my immediate thought was *not again with a bit of fear inside of me.*

His name was Ronald.

He was a well-dressed man who looked like one of those men on the cover of the magazines at the grocery store shelves. Since he frequently came to our house, I was able to semi- adjust to his presence and started to feel semi-comfortable having him around. He was nice though, and he treated my mom, my brother and me well.

We did simple things with him like fishing and shopping, but I often wondered why he would show up only every other week. Was he developing a plan to hurt me too?

Soon, however, I discovered it was because he lived in Riverside, another City in Kentucky.

The first time mom took us to Riverside, I thought that we were *"celebs,"* because the city looked so big compared to where we lived, with its stretched bridges, tall buildings, and different-looking people, not just black and white, but people of different colors.

The only color that I could think of was pink people. Later I found out that they were Asians, and Hispanics.

Getting to his place took forever, but finally when we made it to his house, there was a tall, old, brown building in front of us. It looked like something out of Friday the 13th shows, with Michael Myers looking out the window waiting for us to get out of the car. I was sure that I was a goner this time. Where in the world had my mom taken us to? I wondered.

It was summer break, and I thought that we were being punished or something, because our grades weren't good enough on our report cards, but I had no choice than to get out of the car and walk into this huge building. The walls were old, and dirty.

The staircase to his door took forever to walk up. But to our surprise when we made it up the stairs and the door was finally opened, we walked into a very nice-looking apartment with new furniture.

The whole apartment smelled new, though not as big as where we used to stay at Urbandale.

My brother and I had to share a room, and considering what he had done to me, I was not the happiest person about it. But my brother better keep his distance. I thought to myself, or this is a trip that you will not return from.

We went through our room and we found lots of gifts--a video game, a checker board, playing cards (really? those cards would never be played with nor seen again. I thought to myself) There were new clothes and bikes.

The gifts were sort of a way to make me and my brother feel relaxed and comfortable in our new house. Which it did in a roundabout way of speaking!

We met the neighbor too. She was a very nice pink woman. She spoke ever so softly, and the only word that I can find to describe her is *gentle*. I can't remember her name, but I would like to call her *"Hope."*

Since mom and Ronald often left the apartment and we were not allowed to go out of the building by ourselves, I got to see our friendly neighbor *"Hope"*. She taught me how to make flowers, the plastic kind.

I think that she sold them at a swap meet or nearby mall. Within weeks, I was a real pro at it too. She would take them and sell them all.

"Hope" gave me such peace whenever I was around her. Sometimes I think that *"Hope"* knew what was going on with me, with the looks that she gave me.

Her looks were of warmth, and tenderness. I felt at ease with her. *"Hope"* made my time with her a time of serenity. I was having the time of my life, but wondered just how long it would last. Still, I could have the time of my life with a Snickers Bar and Coca Cola...

My brother and I were really getting used to this life. I was happy for my mom having Ronald then. Ronald and mom went out just about every night, leaving us at the house to pacify ourselves, with our new toys, with me going across the hall to visit *"Hope,"* from time to time.

I would go to see if she was making flowers. Yes, pushovers is what my brother and I were, like little crumb snatchers.

We gobbled up everything. We didn't complain, that is, until our mom came home one night with a black eye and a busted lip.

How could this happen? Ronald was a good person, I thought, and I felt semi-comfortable around him. I couldn't believe this.

I just can't figure out what went wrong between my mom and Ronald. What just happened? I don't understand and there are some things that kids just can't fix, nor can kids know why.

We woke up one early morning to find momma in a haste of packing our clothes and things.

She told us to hurry up and get into the car as fast as we could because Ronald was gone. We needed to leave before he got back. I was truly afraid for my life again. Had something happened to my mom at the hands of Ronald that was so horrible she wanted to protect us from having the same fate as her? It was obvious that she was scared too.

We were only there for a few months, and as soon as we comfortably settled in, our time was up, and we had to go. I never got a chance to say goodbye to my *"Hope,"* but I will never forget her.

Coming back to Urbandale was an easy thing because we knew everyone there, but I will never forget my *"Hope,"* across the hall in Riverside, Kentucky.

Once we were back, what was I to think? Is this the end of my mom's heartfelt emotions, or had she finally changed?

Is my new womanhood causing my mom to show that she cares? Does she really love me now? As a young girl I wondered about all of that. She did try to care for us.

My brother and I wore the best clothes, had the finest apartment, and rode around in top-notch cars. We weren't rich, but somehow mom gave us the best things other kids envy to have.

But what we needed was a mom that we could talk to about anything—our problems, our dreams, our desires and whatnot. I felt I couldn't come to my mom and tell her anything without being judged or being looked at as a little bad-ass hot-tailed girl, just wanting the boys on the block to look at me. Just where was the love? Where was the understanding that a mom is supposed to have for you?

I will never forget *505 Midstream Projects*. Whether it's because it seemed like the end of my world or the beginning of a new journey, I will never forget my life there.

The winter was quickly approaching, and mom told my brother and me that we were moving. We wondered why in the world are we moving again, since we had become so used to living in the projects. I guess that our time was up.

I remember moving into a big house across the tracks by Thurman Rd. This house was right in front of the train tracks. It was a really big house, nothing like granny's house and nothing like the apartment in Midstream Projects. We had a driveway, a grass-filled back yard with shade trees, and a car garage that had a basketball goal already on it.

Were we rich? Did some unknown uncle die and leave us some kind of money so that mom would be at home with us more now? We didn't know, but we were happy. We smiled more often because things seemed to be looking up. *I thought to myself.*

We knew it was going to be the best Christmas ever. I had my own room with a door that closed and locked. I had my privacy and did not have to worry about my brother coming in unannounced.

I didn't have to worry about no one coming in anymore. I could breathe, breathe with my lungs without the assistance of a bag to give me air. Breathe without the feeling of the pillow smothering me from oxygen. I could breathe. I could just lie there and stare at the ceiling and do nothing.

I remember fussing with my brother, because I wanted his room and he wanted mine. But mom had it all laid out. She had gone to Johnson's warehouse and picked out our new bedroom furniture and dining room sets.

Mom was redecorating the whole house to make it into a pleasant and cozy home for me and my brother. She furnished the house in just one evening just for the fun of putting away our new things.

It wasn't even Christmas yet, but we couldn't wait to see what mom had in store for us. It seemed that the heartbreak of Midstream Projects was over and our new mom was here. When I say *new*, it's not like she was old, but something was different, she was renewed.

She acted as if Midstream Projects was history. ***Some things that are history however, always find a way back into our lives.***

She still worked, but not at night anymore. When we came home from school, she was either cooking or pulling in the driveway, as we walked up. Yes, something was different. She was a mom then to us. She started asking us questions about what we liked and what we thought about.

She even played with us from time to time and watched "*Tom and Jerry*," too. She was able to spend time with us, playing, watching and just being there for me and my brother.

November came in and went out fast. The months of winter in Kentucky could be bone chilling cold, as though you could hardly put on enough clothes to keep you warm. It hardly snowed, but it was cold enough to make ice without the help of the fridge.

I know because I did the experiment. I poured water on the back steps one night and then went to bed. My plan was to get up early and check on it to see if it would freeze, but Mom got up before I did, and she found out, yes, it froze. I never admitted to it, but the look on her face when she walked in the house with the mud on the side of her jammers had caused me to giggle and she started laughing with me. That moment, with my mom and me laughing together for such a silly incident was priceless.

In December, mom called my brother and me into the living room and asked what color Christmas tree we wanted. It didn't really matter to us as long as we had presents under it.

But we played along and thought about it and came up with a seven foot tall white tree with true silver and green decorations, with Santa's head at the bottom, so that we could put his milk and cookies there. Even though we knew that the milk and cookies were for mom.

She left and came back with the tree and all the decorations and even lights for the hedges, in the front yard. It was so fun putting the tree up, laughing with mom and my brother trying to get those icicles to lie just right on the branch of the tree. I wish I had taken a picture, but the picture is fixed in my mind.

Just imagine a seven-foot tall white Christmas tree with blue, green and silver décor, icicles, and flashing lights that set off the other colors, as you work your way down, where there's a Santa's head.

The picture that I wanted to stay in my head is the moment my brother and I were doing things with our mom, laughing and being just so happy about it.

It was a couple of weeks away from the big day, Christmas. The whole front room looked like a present factory. I remember thinking that this was going to be a good year and Santa must love us, (wink.)

It was getting late. Mom hadn't come in from work yet. My brother and I were wondering where she was. We heard her car pull up into the driveway. We knew that she was home, but as we looked out the window we saw that someone was with her and wondered who it could be.

Did she go and pick up aunty or granny?

No, she couldn't have because we had just gotten off the phone with them, so we just looked and waited.

She got out of the car and so did the other person and they made their way around to the front door. My brother and I ran to our rooms instead of the door, because we didn't want to look super nosey, even though we were just by the window.

We heard the lock on the door and then the door opened, but we were still asking ourselves who this person could be.

I heard mom calling our names to come in the front room where our Christmas tree was, and like a good boy and girl, we went running—just to see . . . a man standing there with her, and just who was this man?

He couldn't have been a relative, because I had never seen him at any of our family functions, and besides he didn't look like any of us. Then momma said something that shook me to the core.

"You guys," she said, *"This is Randall, and I just wanted for you guys to meet him, because he is going to be coming around from time to time to visit me, okay?"*

We could only look at each other and say, *"OK, Mom."* But my mind was racing. I was praying that this would not be another one of those past nightmares I had with my mom's previous boyfriends. Then he strangely cleared his throat as to say something *like, "Howdy y'all, how y'all doing tonight? Got that school work done?"*

I couldn't help but smile with the tone of his voice. I had never heard such a voice or laughter. He looked funny too and had no teeth with a big toothless smile, but he did something different. He reached out his hand to shake ours, as if being friendly to us.

We shook this stranger's hand and went back into our rooms. Later, my brother came into my room and complained that *"Here we go again—Mom-ma's bringing a man into the house, and every time we are happy she does something like this."*

I strongly agreed with my brother, because this time, whatever was going on between my mom, Andre and I were already good. The three of us were already happy.

This new man in the house had me again feeling uneasy. I was thinking if he comes in here I'm going to kill him because he isn't going to hurt me like her last boyfriend. I slept with a chair behind my door just in case this man wanted to try something. It's a shame that while I was so young I had to have the fear of being hurt surrounding my mind all the time. A few days passed, and then we heard the doorbell.

Looking through the peephole, we saw Randall, but his clothes were different. He looked plain nasty, because mud and dirt covered his pants and shirt. His hands were all black, as though he had been playing with charcoal. He had on a baseball cap that looked as if it were made hundreds of years ago.

Since Momma wasn't home yet from work, I called my brother. He stood next to me as we let Randall in, and he walked in and went straight into Mama's room. He said his *"Howdy,"* of course and once again we just laughed, because his voice sounded so different.

Some time went on, Randall would come and spend the night, take us out to eat and spend time with my brother and me. He'd take us for rides and fishing with mom, when she didn't have to work. We all felt comfortable having each other around.

I even remember that he and mom taught my brother and me how to drive. It was close to my thirteenth birthday that summer, in the Kentucky countryside.

We went down an old country road with nothing to save us if my brother and I drifted over too close to the edge.

Randall just sat us under the wheel and said *"Y'all keep in the middle of this road, because if you go off the edge, I can't get the car out of the ditch."*

Those were fun days. We laughed and played and mom smiled and laughed too. I will never forget those days. Moments that I saw my mom laugh and have fun with us were just priceless.

Some months passed, and we just enjoyed life, the small and big things of it all. But something was unusual. The phone rang more often, and Randall didn't come over as much.

One day, I could hear Momma fussing on the phone, saying, *"Come on, and just bring your ass over here. I wish you would. You're just mad that I got your man. He doesn't want you. Look at you, bitch. I'm waiting outside. You know where I live."*

After listening to all of that, I didn't know just what to think or say because momma looked really upset. I just watched her and said nothing. I felt bad for momma seeing her annoyed and angry. I wish I could do something then.

Randall came over after work looking dirty as usual. He said his hellos and howdy, and did his little funny laugh. My brother and I laughed too, because that voice was too funny.

But Mom-ma's tone was different. They went into the room closing the door. Like any nosey kids, we went to the door to listen.

"Randall, how did she get my number and who does she think she is, calling my house?

My kids were here, and she kept calling. I told her to come over here if she thought that she could do something!"

Randall said, *"Leigh Lee, calm down. She isn't coming over here and she's not going to do anything. You don't have to worry, because I will take care of all of this mess. I don't know why she called you, but I will go over to her house and see why she did."*

My momma replied, *"You better tell her not to call my house again."* It got quiet.

My brother and I looked at each other and then ran. We knew that the door would soon be opening. We had been there listening to the whole conversation.

Sure enough, Randall opened the door and then he left. Trying to figure this one out was really hard. My brother and I wanted to be little gadget Sherlock Holmes type of kids, but it was hard, so we just left it alone and went back to playing basketball in the backyard.

This was only the beginning of many telephone calls and closed door conversations that mom and Randall had. I wasn't that worried with all these closed door conversations, because I could see that after their talks, momma was already okay and smiling. Randall also never argued or even yelled at momma even if momma was yelling at him, because of those annoying calls.

It is just that, after every conversation, Randall didn't stay, but left and came back the next day.

One day the doorbell rang, so we went running, thinking it was Randall coming over.

When we opened the door there was this little old woman standing there. The mere sight frightened me. She had glasses on that looked like someone cut the bottom off of a Coca Cola bottle.

She was wearing a church dress so long that it looked as if she didn't have shoes on and her long, shiny black hair had highlighted her face with such ugliness.

Sorry to have described her this way, but from my eyes, I pictured her to be a present version of a witch from the way she dressed, and painted all that make-up on her face.

We looked at her and then she spoke and said, *"Is Randall here?"*

We were curious who she was and why she was looking for Randall. The thing is, he wasn't at that time, but our mom was.

We screamed for her and she came running, asking *"What's wrong with y'all?"* We responded that there was a woman at the door, and we didn't think that she was an Avon lady. We didn't want to be rude.

However, with that kind of looks, she really was not even suitable to be an Avon lady. My mom was upset seeing her standing at our door. From our mom's eyes, we saw that she knew who she was and that her being there was not good at all. To my mom, her presence was a problem.

She didn't even invite her inside the house. Instead, my mom closed the door, asked us to go to our rooms and they both talked outside. We could hear their voices arguing, but we couldn't understand what it was all about.

When I heard the door open and shut, I knew then that the ugly lady had left. I could hear my mom crying and sobbing at the kitchen. I slowly got out of my room, called my brother and we went to see our mom.

Before getting to the kitchen, she was on the phone with someone. I guess it was Randall she was talking to, since I heard her say, *"Your bitch wife came asking for you,"* and the moment she saw us, she just asked him to come home for dinner. We asked if she was okay, if everything was okay. With a faint smile, she answered yes.

She just told us that the Avon lady gave her a hard time. I gave my mom a hug after that and went with my brother to play.

An hour before dinner time, Randall arrived. He and my mom had a closed door talk again. They got out from my mom's room with Randall holding my mom's hand, as if nothing happened. Then we had dinner the normal way.

My mom was smiling again and Randall was giving us a good dinner chat. I think that was the last time that my brother and I saw this lady.

Not long after that encounter with the lady witch, as I have pictured her in my thoughts, Randall's son, Rover, started coming over to visit Randall. He looked just like Randall and that Avon lady, a combination of both, but of a younger version.

I think I had a crush on him. Well, he made me feel different when he was around. He reminded me of an American Indian, because of his jet black hair, reddish toned skin, and thin build. The type I usually watched on television, about those Indians and how they were in the olden times.

I found them amusing and somehow handsome. The only thing that he was missing was the horse, bow and arrows. I wanted to picture him in my mind as my Indian hero.

I used to make believe that he was my best friend, but he wasn't really. He didn't even know that I existed because when he came to our house, he talked to our mom. His main concern was to talk directly to Randall. He didn't even come inside our house. He just rang the doorbell, asked for Randall, chatted a little with him and my mom then left.

But thanks to my imagination I did see him in a different way. He showed up only on Fridays when Randall got paid. I think he came over to get their share of Randall's salary.

My brother and I decided not to worry about it just as long as mom was happy, that she was not crying, nor hurt, because of Randall or anyone else connected to him. Mom being happy doing things for us and Randall, made us happy.

That creepy Avon lady, witch didn't show up again at our door. That was a relief to me and my brother. Even though my brother and I didn't worry about the creepy Avon lady witch, we knew who she was, she was Randall's wife. We just wondered how our new loving mom could take Randall away from his own family.

The question buzzed around our heads like bees, flying over our heads, but since we were so young, we figured that it wasn't our problem and that mom knew what was best for her and us. What counted most was, that all was well with mom, my brother, me and Randall.

However another unexpected day came. The problem *was* ours again, because Randall came to the house. He started packing up his clothes that he had collected. Then he was gone. Without a word, he just gave me and my brother a hug and left. I could see sadness in his eyes as he was hugging us. I could also feel my eyes forming tears seeing him go.

There were no explanations. Nobody explained about nothing to let us know what happened. Why did it have to be that way? Why did he have to leave?

Again, one of the positive, fun persons to be around, a father figure type, was removed from our lives. I was crushed to see him go, and once again I wondered why. Mom didn't say anything about Randall leaving us. She just continued working, taking care of us and acted as if nothing was changed, except that Randall wasn't there anymore.

The day that he left was the last time we saw Randall at our house. The questions were in my head, but never did I attempt to ask my mom. Not to make it hard on our mom. My brother and I did all we could to make her feel loved, happy and that we were okay without Randall anymore. Inside me, I did miss having him around, having a man in the house that stood as the father of the family. He made us complete in a way, even if we knew he had another family.

We weren't his real family at all. We had to move on now. Now we were returning to my mom, my brother and me once more in the house. All I could hope for is that it would be as happy as it was before Randall had come. We had learned to live through many changes already.

Once more we would do the same thing, going on with our life the way we thought it was going to be until another change came our way. However, no matter what we were left with our memories.

With the departure of Randall, I started missing the man I called father. I began to ask questions to my mom like *"Where is my dad? Why wasn't he in my life?"* *"Doesn't he care for me?"* *"Does he even know that I am alive?"*

For months, all I got was *"Your dad is a good-for-nothing drunk who doesn't care for you, and he never cared for us."*

I think that there are some things that a child shouldn't know. I knew I wasn't that young anymore. I had the right to know the truth about my father and not just what I had heard about him.

I was old enough to know better, so I continued to ask and ask and ask. I know I was already annoying my mom, but I really needed to know. I didn't want to grow up not knowing who my real father was. One day, to my surprise, my mom came into the room and said, *"I have a surprise for you!"*

I asked what it was because I didn't see any gift boxes. Then she said that I was going to see my dad. I got silent, so silent that you could hear the wind blowing outside. I was not expecting this at all. I was caught unprepared for such amazing news.

I never thought she would consider letting me see him, that she would really let me meet my father for real.

"Where is he? Why has it taken him so long?" were the questions that came out from me. She didn't answer those questions. Instead she said that I would have to get on a plane. A PLANE!

I had never been in a plane, nor had I ever seen a plane up close before, just the ones on television. I was so excited and I was having this feeling of euphoria. I made sure that I told everyone that I came into contact with starting with my granny, my aunty, and my uncles, but they already knew.

I did remember that there was a time my aunt sat me down and talked to me and said it's time for you to know just where and who you came from. I just didn't understand it back then, what was she saying, but later I would find out.

When the day to meet my father came closer, mom bought me all new clothes for the trip and packed my suitcase. She made sure I was ready to leave. Then one sunny morning, we went to Grand View. I wondered if David, my dad, and my mom were playing a trick on me, but they weren't.

The day finally had come when my mom took me to get onto a plane to meet my father. We arrived at the airport, and I was in heaven watching the planes take off and land. I can't explain fully the feeling I was having inside, seeing the planes up close, or was it the feeling of finally getting to meet my father.

Then my mom came to me and asked if I was OK, of course I wasn't. I was nervous and scared, and to make it even worse, I was getting on it alone. I had never been in a plane, but what mattered most was going to see my dad.

Not the men that mom brought home, who played the role of a dad to me. I told her bravely that I was fine and ready to go. I didn't know much about the world, but wherever Detroit was, I was going. I was determined to go. I didn't know just how long it would take to get there.

But I was ready to do whatever it took to pass the time just as long as I got to see and be with my dad. I wanted to be with the man that I had longed for and needed to know. This was the man that I truly wanted to have in my life. He had been missing for so long from life.

The airline was southwest, and I remember that from the colors of the plane, which are brown and orange.

As I walked up the walkway to the plane, I looked down and I could see the ground. I figured that I was really high up in the air. I began to get nervous.

I could feel my knees trembling as I boarded the plane. I was then assisted inside by the pretty ladies dressed in such elegant clothes. Seeing that I was with no one, the flight attendant was nice to me, as she guided me to my seat.

She kept asking me if I wanted peanuts and peanuts and more peanuts. She put my seat-belt on and asked me not to take it off until the pilot told me to. She said that if I had to go to the bathroom, all I had to do was just wave at her to let her know. She would take me there. I listened to her very carefully. I figured she knew what she was talking about and cared for my safety.

The plane was soon backing up, and as I looked out the window I could see my mom standing there wiping tears from her eyes. I knew this was hard on her, to see me go, leaving her and my brother.

But at my age and with all the longing for a father, the excitement had me waving and smiling. I just had the feeling that I was ready to go. Once the backup was complete, we began to go forward and turned, turned again, then suddenly stopped. A voice came over the air saying, *"This is your captain."* That's all I remember. When he was finished, I remember my head going back into the seat like being on a carnival ride. I felt as if my feet were off the ground.

Up! Up, up, up!

I looked out the window to see where we were. All I could see were clouds, more clouds, little buildings and ants that I later found out were cars. I began to feel ill. I could feel butterflies in my stomach until the time I drifted off to sleep. I woke up to a big jerk. I came off the seat and went forward.

I got a bit scared and was startled from the plane's sudden jerk. I thought I was having a dream until the flight attendant came over and asked if I was okay.

"What is wrong? Is everything okay," I said. She replied that nothing was wrong. That everything was okay and that the plane had just landed, which sometimes caused a jerk. She undid my seat-belt and asked me if I knew who I was going to see.

I explained that I was going to meet my dad for the very first time after years of not knowing him, and that I didn't know how he looked.

She assured me that I would know when I saw him and led me back down the long walkway and into a big room. She gathered my suitcases, and then a nice man pushed them behind us. As we were walking, she knew where to go.

I noticed four people walking towards us and pointing at me. As we got closer to them, I didn't know why, but I had a gut feeling. I could tell that the shortest man looked like me, just a bright-skinned version though.

I knew deep inside me that he was my dad. I could feel my blood rushing, as I began to run towards him, like dogs were chasing me, like a fire was trying to burn me up. I ran as fast as I could and jumped, wrapping my arms around him, just as he said, *"Lana Marie, I love you."*

Tears poured down my face, tears of joy, tears of hope, and tears of great happiness, as I finally saw my dad. I could feel my heart beating so fast from the moment my dad's hand held mine.

From the moment I saw my dad, I didn't want to let him go. I held tight to his hand.

I also met my aunty Jean, her husband, Uncle Ray, and my Paw paw, Charlie. In an instant, I had met a new family that I never knew I had. I immediately felt totally loved by them.

The airport was nothing like Grand View's back in Kentucky. It was huge, with really big stairs that moved up and down. It even had more planes. They were taking off and landing, as I walked hand in hand with my dad.

The sun was shining bright like it never had before. I think even God was shining down on me, because I was so happy on that day, at that very moment in time.

I have never seen so many cars before. My eyes were big and wide seeing all these things. It was like so surreal to me to be in such a bigger city.

How they found their car in that maze-like parking lot was a big puzzle to me, but that was the least of my worries.

I didn't even care about how my hair looked, nor how the weather was because it was hot, hotter than the sun. I think, at least that's how it felt at that moment. My dad didn't say much.

He held my hand and looked into my eyes, as if he could see my soul, feel my pain, and answer the questions that were in my head, without me saying a word.

As I looked at him, one of the first things that I thought is *so* that's where I got this nose, my hair color, and my eyes.

I was thinking he could never deny me, because of this nose. Funny that I thought not too many people in this world could have a nose like this, but I would soon see that I was wrong.

After spending forever on the plane and forever in the car gazing at my dad, we finally made it to aunty Jean's and Uncle Ray's house on Mint Frost Rd. As the car pulled up the driveway, a cluster of people came out of the house, as though the house was about to burst into flames.

They were my family as well. There were uncles, aunts, cousins, and even another brother. Tiny was his name. He looked like me and had that same nose too.

I didn't imagine that I would have this many family members in this part of the world. I only had thought of having my family in Newburgh Street.

Dad, I, Uncle Ray and Aunt Jean all walked into a room in the house and sat down. I had so many things to tell my dad. I didn't know which to say first. I knew my dad felt the same way.

Then my Dad told me *"Lana Marie, I am the happiest man on earth right now. I never thought that Leigh would ever let you come see me."*

I asked him why he wasn't ever there for me, when so many bad things happened to me. I needed him. He said that he knew about what had happened. He was sorry about what that man had done to me. He asked if I had received the letters that he had written me. Letters that I had never knew anything about. Letters my mom never spoke of or even gave to me.

When he asked about the money he sent, my jaw dropped. *"You sent me money too?"* I said.

Tears once again rolled down my face. Somehow, when I hadn't met him yet, I had bad feelings towards him.

I hated him for leaving me alone with my mom, letting all those bad things happen to me. I felt he never cared. I thought he never loved me. But all those thoughts against him were wrong. I was so wrong!

My dad cared and my mom had never told me. My dad gently wiped my tears away and gave me a big, comforting hug, saying *"Don't cry, Lana Marie, I am here and I will never leave you again."*

He went on to say that he and my mom were married and were still married when I was born, but he cheated on my mom with another women. Then he started drinking. He explained that drinking took over his life, but not one day went by that he didn't think about me and how he was going to see his baby girl again.

His cheating and drinking had pushed my mom to leave him. He also said that my mom didn't want him to be in my life. That I didn't need him. He went on to say that she told him to drop off the face of the earth, because I would never see him and he would never see me.

We both knew that promise was one that she could not keep, because I was with him. I knew then my dad loved me so much. He loved me, not like the love that I got from my mom, but like the love a child can only feel from a father. A feeling that words couldn't describe.

When we walked out of the room holding hands, nothing and no one could break me away from him. I sat on his lap like a little kid with all smiles. Then everyone said, let's go to the back yard.

When I opened the sliding glass door, the aroma of barbecue hit my nose. You could hear lively music playing, people enjoying their food, and more family members to meet.

There was a bunch of colorful balloons and a banner that read "Welcome Home and Happy Birthday!" I cried uncontrollably. I almost forgot that it was my birthday!

I was fourteen years old and I received one of the greatest gifts I could have ever asked for, my dad was there with me. My dad held my hand even tighter and assured me that it would be okay. He told me to just relax and get to know our family.

I was introduced to everybody who was there. I was Lana Marie, the daughter of David Thompson. I was acknowledged finally, by my dad as his daughter. I had a blast once I relaxed.

I had one cousin named Yoli, that I connected with more than the others and I love that girl. She was a few years younger than I, so it was like having a little sister. I never had a sister feeling with anyone, but it's like she and I meshed thick as thieves. In all the fourteen years of my life, this was the best birthday I ever had.

Then I was off to the hair salon, the malls, the barbeque's, more malls, shoe stores, and walks on the famous downtown strip where I fell in love with shrimp cocktail and bright lights.

Wherever we went, I felt secure and cozy, because in every adventure, my dad was holding my hand, and at the same time he gave me a smile. It was only a smile that he and I had, and I felt reassured that nothing and no one would hurt me.

During the four months I spent in Detroit, that memory is the only thing burnt into my memory. Nothing else mattered. (Or did it? You never know what God's intentions are for you in life until life starts to unfold.)

Eventually my time in Detroit came to an end, and it was time for me to return to Kentucky. I hadn't had enough moments with my dad. The four months flew past so quickly that it was just like four days to me. I wanted to stay longer. I wanted time to move so very slow.

I didn't want to return, but my dad called my mom and she said that I had to. He sat me down once again and said not to worry, that I would come back before I knew it. The flight back was a very sad one for me, I didn't want to leave my new family or the people that I was just now beginning to know and love.

Once again I had to drift off to sleepy land with the feeling of sadness and once again was awakened by a jerk to find myself back in Grandview, Kentucky.

I wasn't that happy to see my mom. I remembered all that my dad told me. He had continuously make contact with her and even with me. However, my mom had decided to hide everything from me. She stole that truth away from me. I didn't smile or hug her. She looked at me and said *"You've changed,"* and I simply said, *"Yes, I have."* I had hatred for her.

The ride back in the car was a quiet one. I didn't have too many words to say to my mom. What I was thinking in my head was pure hatred for her, but it could never come out. The drive took us close to three hours to make it back to Urbandale, but the three hours felt like thirty hours.

Once we pulled up, I saw my older brother and ran and hugged him just as I did with my father. He was still my safety net, my rock and my shelter from the storms that tried to take me from time to time. He and I walked and talked about Detroit for hours.

He commented about my hair cut, since half of my hair was cut out. It was the style in Detroit, but looked like an alien in Kentucky. What can I say? Sugar "n" Spice was "in" those days, and I loved that music group.

My silence and coldness to my mom had grown stronger and deeper. I wanted to blame her for everything that had happened to me. I wanted to blame her, because if she hadn't hide the truth about my father, I would not have lost my innocence in such a horrible way.

My mom's attitude was different as well. One day she asked me to clean the kitchen, and I said I would clean it later, because it was that curse time of the month, and I didn't feel good. Without any warning, she walked up to me and slapped my face and said, *"Bitch."*

She repeated, *"Go and clean that kitchen. You're just like your no good ass daddy, and you ain't shit and will never be shit."* Her words were like knives carving the flesh off of my heart. I never felt so hurt. But I can't fight my mom because I still am my granny's daughter at heart.

I still respected her even if I hated her that much. I had never run away from my mom, except for that day.

I ran to the train tracks, by the recycle center down the street. I knew she couldn't find me because of all of the old cars and piles that were around. I stayed there hidden until night fell. I had stopped crying. Then I walked back.

The house was dark when I opened the door, but my brother was there. He was waiting for me and he came up to me and asked if I was okay. He didn't understand why mom said that to me, neither did I.

I don't know why my mom hated my dad so much, that she took her anger for him out on me. I should be the one to be angry at her, right?

My brother promised and said to me that night that he would protect me from her and not to worry. If he were only twelve feet tall and five hundred pounds, then he could save me.

My mom soon returned, but I was fast asleep, or at least I pretended to be fast asleep, I should say.

I could hear my brother talking to her, asking her how could she say those things to me and treat me that way and her response was, *"You're a child, so stay in a child's place."*

Then he firmly said *"You're not hitting my sister again."*

When morning came, mom was gone, and it was peaches and ice cream all day long. Yes, peaches and ice cream, was our favorite breakfast and lunch.

We would eat while outside playing basketball and making a tree house for me to escape to, from my mom. We figured that mom couldn't climb trees to get to me. It was my safe haven for many nights.

I heard over and over again that I wasn't shit, that I wasn't going to amount to anything, that I was no good and that I was going to be like my Aunt Jean. Repeatedly and non-stop my mom said all those words to me every chance she could possibly say it to my face.

Those words would break down even the strongest-willed person or adult. I was a teenager. I knew that no child should be treated in that manner. I wanted to leave my mom. I hated her so much. But I was thinking of my brother.

So, I just let the memories of my father and the time I was in Detroit keep me on my feet helping me to be a strong child. The time where all the family showed their love and cared, especially my dad.

School started, and when the first batch of report cards came out, the teacher handed me mine. I saw a "D". I needed to make the "D" look like a "B" or something.

I knew my mom would surely be so angry at me, but I didn't. I just said that my mom wouldn't ask us for them, so I told my brother about the "D."

He said, just tell her about the hard time that I was having in the class and that she would understand, so we went home and began our homework. Shortly after mom came in, I looked at my brother. He looked at me, and we didn't say anything.

I walked into my room and then my mom asked for me to come to where she was, so I did. She asked for the report card. As I expected, when she saw the "D" she flipped out and said "no phone, no new clothes, no allowance, nothing." I wondered why since I had only one "D" and the rest were "A's" and "B's."

Then I said "My brother has mostly "C" grades, so why are you treating me like this?" Then she said, *"Don't worry about your brother, worry about yourself"*, and I said *"That's not fair! What did I do to you?"* Out of my frustrations for not knowing why my mom couldn't seem to understand me. I couldn't also understand why she treated me that way. I went to get the dictionary and then dropped it onto the table. It did made a banging sound.

Out of nonsense anger, she grabbed my hair and punched me in my face. The blood trickled down my nose, and she kept hitting and hitting me, since she was my mom I didn't want to hit her back. I tried protecting my face with my hands, as I struggled to get away and run out of the house saying *"I hate you, I hate that I am your daughter, and I don't ever want to see you again."*

I ran all the way to my uncle's house further down the street. When I knocked on his door, he opened it as if he knew that it was me. He was so surprised to see my face covered in blood. I walked in, and as soon as I walked in, the phone rang. Then my uncle said, *"She's here, and don't worry about her. I am calling the police. Why would you beat your child like this? You are no sister of mine–I disown you."*

Not too long after that, while my uncle was cleaning up my blood-covered face and trying to put medicine to my wounds, a car pulled up. It was my granny. She walked in and looked at my face, picked up the phone angrily and called my mom and said, *"If you ever hit this girl like this again, I will kill you. Do you understand me?"*

I guess my mom asked where I was and said that she wanted to speak with me, but my granny said *"No, you aren't talking to her."*

Then my granny sat me down and told me that she was sorry that my mom did this to me. She didn't raise her like this, and she didn't understand how a mom could do this to her own child. They couldn't understand why mom was acting this way towards me.

My granny said that she never stopped reminding mom to treat us right for we were her own children, especially me, who had been through a lot because of the people she was involved with.

She went on to say that she knew about how my mom was treating me, and the things she was saying to me. I asked how she knew this, and she said *"Your brother calls me all the time and we talk, and he cries as he talks to me about the way your mom is treating you."*

I began to cry and my granny tried to assure me that it wouldn't happen again. I spent a few days at my uncle's house, so that my wounds could heal, because I couldn't go to school with a face all messed up.

When the time came for me to return home, my granny showed up with my aunty and my other uncle. Then all of us went to my mom's house.

The ride took only a few minutes and it was quiet, eerily quiet. Then we made it to the house and just walking up there made me ill. I wanted to back out and ran away again. But my granny gave me the look of assurance.

I cried and didn't want to walk in, but my granny grabbed my hand and said that I would be all right. I wanted to believe her, but my heart of hearts knew that it wouldn't be.

As we walked in, my brother was standing there, and he walked up to me and asked if I was okay. I said no, because I didn't want to be there. He said that he understood and he was sorry that he couldn't save me from her. My brother felt so sorry for me. We hugged and I felt the love from my brother. My granny then told us to go into the back room and watch television, so that she and my uncles could talk to my mom.

But even though we were in the back room, we could still hear them talking *"Leigh Lee, what's wrong with you?"* I could hear my granny say. *"Why did you do this to her? You need help, and if you ever do this again, we will kill you. "*

"I have my shotgun in the trunk of that car out there, and I swear that if you hurt that child again, you will pay for it with your life. Do you understand me?"

Then I heard mom say, *"Yes"* and that she was really sorry for hurting me. When my granny called me into the room, my mom then stood up and gave me a hug that I didn't want to receive, but I felt that I had to. I cried as mom held me in her arms, but I knew deep inside me that I would never forget what she did. I would not forget all the pain and suffering that I had encountered caused by her selfishness.

I would not forget the lies and hurtful words she said about my father. My life would never be the same again. Then my granny and uncles left.

A couple of days passed, and my mom called my brother and me into the room and told us that we were moving AGAIN!

This again, will be another unknown chapter of my life. New place - new people - another change. I just prayed and I just hope it wouldn't be as traumatic and cruel as it was the last time. However, the unknown fear was present and my brother and I would look out for each other no matter what was to come.

www.ingramcontent.com/pod-product-compliance
Lightning Source LLC
Chambersburg PA
CBHW060622130626
46555CB00002B/615